Purple Men 2000

Robert Glück

Published in London by Ssnake Press, 2025

© Robert Glück 2003

Originally published in 2003 by Clear Cut Press in the collection *Denny Smith*

Cover art by Jazmin Key

ISBN 978-1-068-47882-6

Purple Men 2000

for Loring McAlpin

THEY WAKE UP

The next time Trent wakes up it's 4 a.m. on Wednesday, August 4, 1993. Therapists prepare us for death and Morrissey just released his third solo album. It's not very dark—tree shadows rotate on the curtains. Trent hears sharp yelping and drones from the bedroom of his neighbor below. Albie is a Korean bodybuilder whose lover died a few months before. Albie is cheerful during the day but weeps without restraint in the early hours. His weeping comforts Trent. It means that love is something, that Trent can love like a mortal and cry whole-heartedly when Daryl dies.

Daryl and Trent are still together. Their bodies spoon a few hours later, the twisted sheet coiling around their thighs. I depend on them to stay together: held in the middle distance and then tipped out of it.

The fog-muted light casts soft rectangles on the curtains and birds chatter in the old plum tree. After three scorching days, the heat is abating. On Sunday it was 98 degrees, the hottest August 1st since 1849.

Daryl backs onto an elbow to watch over the glory of Trent's waking. Trent seems motionless till Daryl quiets his attention. Activity builds in stages: eyes roving under lids, pulse ticking in the neck, belly filling with air, penis adjusting. Daryl is drunk with tenderness and fear that perfection ends. The thin skin jumps over Trent's heart. His sour breath, his big feet with their splayed toes, the taut milky skin around his navel, his lofty brow: Daryl laughs with the joy of possession.

Daryl is so intent he doesn't notice that Trent is feeling at home in consciousness. "Look," Trent pats his erection, "nature's toothbrush."

"Quite a come-on," Daryl whispers. "Have much success with that line? Would I be surprised?"

"Pissrod? Fuckpole?" Trent asks his member. He feels pleasantly filled up. Daryl and Trent have been together since 1977; they marvel at that. They were banished by chance from an impersonal Golden Age but they conserve the era before chance in a private religion. Put another way, they are children who acquired language: their first triumphs long past, they are diminished by the clumsy medium. Ed, Frank, and Sharon died; Rick, Sam, and Larry moved to New York. Others just drifted away, leaving Daryl and Trent somewhat isolated. These friends were not replaced; instead, the need to be reflected in the psyche of others subsided. When that need emerges, they have a party. A dinner.

"911-RUB," Trent says.

"I already jacked off," Daryl admits pallidly. He was wakeful with excitement about the duck he's going to braise for the dinner party so he masturbated twice during the night to get back to sleep. Their dear legs and thighs are packed in salt and thyme in the refrigerator.

"You came? I don't want you to get ahead of me," Trent scolds, as though he's keeping track. Trent embodies the good points of San Francisco: beauty and disposition. Daryl is like the city's culture: community-driven, anarchistic, insecure. Sixteen years of mutual description exaggerate these traits. Trent is a gardener who works his own route and Daryl is about to earn $48,000 a year writing technical manuals for Oracle. He's floating through the week between orientation and work.

They live like their friends—with some nice things, good equipment, restaurant meals. They solve the problem of one thing happening after another by watching TV and going to movies. They solve the problem of individual life by giving it away. Like everyone else, they dumb down, a willing degradation exciting as summer blockbusters where narration itself seems to perish in spectacular last breaths. The are extremely underinsured.

Daryl says, "Let's stay in bed and never leave. We'll order out, pizza and Chinese. We'll grow fat like two baked apples—"

Daryl could have made this wish any time during the last sixteen years, but Trent sees fear in Daryl's random jokes since Daryl was diagnosed; even Daryl does, reading his own mind. Actually he was thinking about the dreary orientation and the yellow legal tablets stacked in the center of a big round table. No one could reach them. Daryl's longing for a tablet distracted him all day, like a cake out of reach.

Daryl fares into the kitchen. He pauses a moment to smell his own sweet warmth in the cooler air. He feels still; inside of that, orbits whir like a gyroscope. He's pale beneath dusky skin; his amber eyes and straight black eyebrows stand out since he buzzed his hair to outsmart his bald spot. Black fuzz grows across his belly, a thin mat covers his chest, curls sprout on his butt—a proto-bear, scratchy outside, hot and slippery within.

He feels new to the room, exposed. He puts the water on and runs crouching out the front door and down the steps to retrieve the *Chronicle*. Someone tucked a manila envelope in the newspaper. Daryl turns quickly: backs are less naked than fronts and he wants to hide his nascent belly. He hates it but can't prevent it even though, guided by Albie, he progressed from Nautilus to free weights at the gym. Daryl hopes his new muscles will fight the virus.

The kettle groans, the water beats a tattoo on the metal walls, the whistle mounts frantically. Daryl pours the sputtering stream into the clay pot—an ageless consoling gesture like folding cloth. In 1993, according to the community's self-description, there are two modes of gay masculinity: a young, sexy sick white man and a young, sexy healthy white man. To be precisely a community's self-description is a kind of immortality. Daryl is thirty-six, an old young man, older than he wants to be for the first time. Age drags him off the personals page of the *Bay Times*, which accommodates so many other variations. Soon age will shunt him down to the short column at the end—*Daddy Seeking.*

Trent is thirty-three, still eternally young. A force larger than himself carries him to theme orgies discovered on the Internet and parties where he unironically becomes a probation officer or a horse. He's not really into S/M though he's been tied up. If anyone is "serious" about performing some act on his body, he doesn't flinch, recognizing the call of a higher order. To Daryl, Trent seems always new, always arriving from some stranger's embrace which baptizes his flesh.

Trent longs to fuck without a condom. He hasn't lost close friends—they were Daryl's. If anything, the support groups snare Trent in the web of relation so by the time an acquaintance finally dies he is a friend.

Trent was a waiter, a janitor, and a light carpenter. When Daryl tried hiring CHOKE ON THIS! from the back pages of the *B.A.R.*, he learned that Trent also worked as an erotic dancer/prostitute. Unreally, Daryl heard CHOKE's greeting from the receiver in one ear and from the kitchen in the other.

"Is that you, Trent?"

Daryl was demonstrating a kind of fidelity, Trent felt, if only to body type. "Sex work is a social responsibility, like the Peace Corps or jury duty," he piously asserted into the phone and down the hall. Finally Daryl put his foot down. Trent and Joyce, their couples counselor, exclaimed, "Daryl made a demand!" Trent was glad to stop. He was tired of jacking off in old men's faces, plus he was a decade older than his peers, who were putting themselves through the San Francisco Art Institute.

The pale golden room emanates from Trent's skin. Daryl opens the curtains and waggles his cock at the psychiatrist who built a tall house that shades their garden half the year.

Trent hisses, "Daryl!"

"Why should *we* hide in *our* home because *he* built *five* windows on the *property* line?" The horrid doctor's gray head darts upward to get a better look and downward to stay hidden. Daryl's insult is legible to the snoop.

The tea is steeped, its fragrance a pure note. Daryl brings two cups back to bed along with the newspaper and the envelope. Trent entirely welcomes the tea, Daryl, the allegory of domesticity, and the silk of his drowsy body. Unlike every other man, Trent is certain he made the right commitment. Gertrude Stein wrote, "There is nothing inevitably different between being a boy and a man in a frenchman's life and he is always a son because he is always dependent upon his mother for his strength his morality, his hope and his despair, his future and his past." That's how Trent depends on Daryl.

Trent picks up the manila envelope. He recognizes Ron's...aura. Trent has not heard from Ron since New Year's Eve, when the front door was smeared with shit. He sniffs the envelope. "Let him be dead," Trent prays. They met at The Hole in the Wall in the mid-eighties and started necking against the jukebox. *Bang bang on the door/Love shack baby...* The bartender mildly asked them not to crush the glass but Ron was affronted. Trent followed him on unsteady legs through the crowd, proud and ashamed. There was something off-kilter about Ron, his thin lips and long hectic cheeks. They began necking at My Place. They were just mouths urgently scrolling inside each other. Now in a daydream Trent turns a table over and kicks Ron in the head.

Trent was a janitor. He found Ron a studio but Ron declined to pay rent. He complained to Trent about the studio's defects; later he complained about Trent's defects, never stopping, but telling Trent in new ways exactly how he was a human dud. Ron's lips drew back from his bitter words. Trent listened with a puzzled expression as though through a language barrier. He said, "So, uh, some lunch?" Ron was evicted after two years of legal obstruction—his insane, successful suit against the building's owner. Ron demonizes Trent as the fiend of that eviction.

"Breathing in is witchcraft. Your vanity is the curse of Nefertiti that separates life into night and day. Aliens killed her—" They read the horrific anonymous letter, written in red crayon between glued fragments of eviction notice.

"Wow," Daryl says. "My boyfriend is the Antichrist! The Antichrist *would* be a big blond."

"And an enemy of all artists. Ron thinks he's an artist. The arms on the swastikas are backwards," Trent notes.

"Ron *is* an artist—look at this page." Replying to Trent's expression Daryl adds, "Of course I mean artist disparagingly."

"He says the garden looks nice. So he's watching the house? Should I call the police?"

To interest the police, Trent must catch Ron in the act of smearing excrement on the door or stabbing him in the heart. Instead, Trent checks on his sick fish. Daryl puts three fat cookbooks in Trent's place and begins a shopping list for their dinner party on a yellow legal tablet.

SORRY DOESN'T FIX IT

The fishbowl is quick and alive, like a fountain in the living room. When it was time to choose, Trent rejected the brilliant fish darting from one side of the tank to the other. He pointed to a dun lionhead that lumbered peaceful as a blimp. The clerk said, "Her?" Her ocher splotch and muted browns matched the castle. As an afterthought, Trent chose a gold koi to honor tradition and to own a bauble. Her fins were golden scarves.

Daryl said, "Let's name them."

"They're Francie and Cleo," Trent replied as though merely reminding him.

Francie's face was sweet and calm. She was happy in her gallon and hung out in the portal of the castle, which was gratifying. Cleo, the conventional beauty, circled without respite, rattling the bars of her cage. She *never* entered the castle; *la prisonnière* would not accept Trent's hospitality or consent to the terms of her confinement. Maybe under water the filter's bubbles sounded like an angry hive: *make it stop make it stop make it stop*. Although her body was no bigger than Francie's, her long fins seemed to knock everything over.

It seemed to Trent that Cleo was vain, with her long skirts, metallic body and doe eyes. Her intensity was discouraging. Were the two fish friends?—or did Francie's motion spur motion in Cleo and vice versa? The pet store guy talked as though they were little machines. Sometimes one tried to push the other to the surface—was that play or shoving your roommate off a cliff? These bouts started after eating, when fights erupted in Trent's family.

Francie enjoys timelessness, but Cleo had episodes. She sank to the bottom, just breathing. After a few weeks, she hung vertically in the water, a tangerine wedge. Then she nested in the seaweed like a bird. It gave the bowl a haunted feeling. Yesterday, she began to fight the surface, a soul struggling to remain in her element. The owner of the fish store gave Trent some salt to heal her infected air bladder, which he diagnosed. Trent stirred a teaspoon into the bowl along with drops that dyed the water blue.

Now Cleo gads about the castle but Francie slows down. Fewer gulps, fewer heartbeats: departing from life by experiencing it less and less. Although most things can't be known, this slowing down is recognizable. She lingers in a corner that Cleo doesn't visit. Francie's yawning, yawning. Some part of Trent slows down, slows down. He feels as immobilized as Roderick Usher—what can he *do* for Francie in her coffin fishbowl nightmare? Trent is scared. Francie deflates as life passes out of her. He tries to push her spirit back with the force of his concern. He thinks with anguish, "I've marinated her, or is that pickling?"

It's strange how you know immediately when someone dies. The breathless corpse steals the air.

Francie lists slightly and sways with the current. *Oh my god she's dead through no fault of her own the one I loved!* Francie leaves no will: the castle, the black sand, the string of seaweed—

Trent feels the horror of a corpse, its flat-tipped eyes. What implement to use?—a mesh strainer with a handle, a kitchen tool. It gives him the willies but he reasons, Dead fish are not strangers to the kitchen. Out of the bowl Francie is smaller, wilted. Human corpses seem bigger. Her poor body flies clockwise downward. Even now Trent expects it to switch back on. The little carp's watery grave—down down to Davy Jones' Locker. In five seconds the body is gone forever.

Trent doesn't turn the filter off—it sputters and bubbles for no reason. "Oh, to keep Cleo alive," Trent reminds himself bitterly. "Then how do you go on living?"—he says to the fishbowl. "Globally," he laments, "and in smaller and smaller fragments."

Trent is late. He dresses for work, his end-of-Act-Up outfit: baggy jeans, faded t-shirt, Doc Martens, backwards baseball cap. Daryl lies in bed with his cookbooks. He catches the moment when Trent buttons his pants with a turn and the bunched cloth falls into shape against his narrow waist and wide rump. Before Trent leaves, he pockets the long shopping list Daryl made for dinner and eats a few stalks of leftover asparagus to flavor his cum.

TYPICAL EXISTENCE

The morning fog burns off and there's salt in the mild breeze. The heat wave is over. Trent jumps into his green pickup and shifts the arthritic gears. The truck smells sweetly of manure.

Twitter Chatterley's large yard climbs a hill: her decks and garden rooms are reached by steep cement paths and stairs. It's an estate garden in miniature. Trent controls scale and color while his blowzy plantings and mounds of gray foliage create an overgrown look. The treble and bass of a fountain. Trent thinks, Fish don't have retention spans—the bowl is an expanding universe.

Trent stumbles on Bill the butler. He's in white shorts, lolling on a chaise. He looks up from the *Chronicle* and advises, "Keep secrets to yourself, Leo. Make time for a special friend." His orange hair glows in the soupy light. Sounds blurt and disappear. A spindly eucalyptus keeps this corner of the garden sunless; it rhymes with Bill's enclosed nature.

The insides of Bill's thighs are white, larval. Wasps circle, or skinny bees. Buzzzzzz: the sound of pleasure and distress. They land on Bill's skin, crawl a few inches, take off. Trent is exasperated. He wants to ask Bill if he gets stung but doesn't want to give that to Bill, wants to barely notice him. He thinks, There's a creepy man/woman tension, like the bees are supposed to scare us girls. The mansion, hidden in a crowded city, resembles a run-down plantation.

Vines brought Trent here. Reporting on Bay Area vines for a community college horticulture class, he discovered house and butler. There's no hive. Could they live in the ground?

Bill removes his white bucks and ivory socks and wiggles his triangular toes. He carries his shoes away, but reappears shirtless, bringing a bottle of beer for Trent on a little silver tray. There isn't much to do in August. Delighting in perfectly dispensable action, Trent soaks the pots of annuals dried out by the heat wave and fertilizes the orchids. He deadheads some *pelargonium sidoides*, a plant for the nineties: green-gray foliage and dark violet spiky blooms. In the sun the garden is almost animated. Two white butterflies orbit each other and a hummingbird talks to him with its plangent voice from its perch in the dazzling light. Trent's clefts and bulges detain beads of sweat. Magnificent Trent, the birthday candle of his generation proclaiming the nothingness of flesh by displaying its glory.

Trent deadheads and fertilizes the frayed cream-and-yellow roses. He sweeps the cement paths until he chances on Bill loitering beneath the orange brugmansia. Bill zigzags toward Trent with a strange dip as though stepping into a slow dance. He slips his hand over Trent's crotch, "Is that a wocket in your pocket?" There is nothing to undo but the drawstring of Bill's bathing suit whose orange and purple stripes swell outward.

Bill's red penis hoists itself into the air by

degrees as Bill waits placid and shameless as a dog, big-faced, shallow-eyed and panting. For the moment Trent is Ms. Chatterley's butler's lover. Bill escorts the elderly Twitter to the opera, charity dinners and such. Fashionable Twitter perching on the arm of a young fag drawn to her in class-need stronger than sex. Trent is not Bill's lover any more than Paolo the indoor gardener, Dirk the chauffeur, or Aaron the handyman.

It's painful to see such a hard-working muscle fastened to so slender a frame. There's little to Bill besides penetration. He shaves his balls and the bottom of his pubes; a red poof hovers above. Trent has a weird shift in scale, Bill is a midget with average genitals, his balls drape like a pink apron. Trent doesn't take his shirt off—just drops his jeans. One naked man is enough. It's funny to send his cock outside, the unusual warmth, Mr. Sun.

Trent enters the sex slowly. He's distracted by a white glass cup someone left above them on the old railing of a deck extending from the back of the house. Light glows through the cup and darkens its outline, detaching it from two of its four dimensions. Amid the urgency of flower and fruit, the cup's clarity, humility, and the likelihood that it was forgotten make it fiercely beautiful. Life promises more life by quickly replacing one image with another image, yet here is an image that seems to be an end, like Albie's tears.

A rich silence overwhelms the random

chirps, buzzes, rustling, and electric drones. The night-scented brugmansia's orange trumpets emit a faint daytime fragrance, gardenia with edge. Trent has this inkling: the world is radical but just beyond his reach because society keeps him slightly crazed, promoting a mild insanity to distract him—from what?

They turn their legs out so their hips open and their cocks stand. Bill says, "You should thank Mother Nature every day of your life." After a while, their attention becomes that stance, the sheer drop from chest to groin—the body composed—then a countermovement, flesh vulnerable and questing. An erect cock is an abnormal thrill. Although Bill is slight, he's lush when embraced, the sweetness of flesh packed tight. Turning him around, the crack of Bill's small ass leads upward to a valley of thin bruised skin that looks painfully new. Desolate vale—sexy in its unsuccessful joining.

Bill has this feeling: that the inside of Trent's body is continuous with its exterior. Trent is like a porn star; he cancels his own spongy, pressured, gooey, tight, gassy, inner sensations and becomes his own lust and also Bill's. For Bill, sex is a club to clobber beauty with. The scent of Trent's body rises in waves. A mosquito hums; it drops on Bill's little rump and Trent swats it neatly, a blood valentine.

Bill takes pride in the art of the blowjob. He has subdued his gag reflex, which requires focus and self-discipline. Trent nods approvingly, but he is unwilling to be distracted from the cup that seems to halt sight and conduct him to the inexhaustible clarity of the world. Trent's body leads its own life, its twin chefs cook the small meal, while he wishes for a different kind of eternity.

Trent thinks, Is this *my* sensation? Methodical suction disorders him. His cock is the world's whole reality for Bill during the time it takes to make it come. Trent views the top of Bill's orange head and translucent ears from a lofty tenderness, but his orgasm isolates him. He bats his forehead as though putting out a fire, then becomes a Y, victorious arms and frazzled expression, a runner breaking the tape at the finish line. Trent would not be so dramatic if Bill were looking.

The blaze that is Trent is not comfortable to experience from the inside. In Trent it's high summer, he's peaking, the buzzing of insects is glory without relief. His B.O. is so intense he feels it on his face, olfactory blushing. Bill sweats through his nose and the soles of his feet like a dog. The butler thinks, After a blowjob there is nothing to clean up. He stumbles, tipsy on sperm, and Trent can taste the flat scum on Bill's breath along with a sulfuric dash of asparagus.

It's understood: No kissing. With kisses there's a plotline, a question of fidelity. Bill says, "Milk me, Sugar." For some reason he always says that. Trent gapes, exactly the effect Bill wants. Trent feels quick sporadic movements. Bill's orgasm is just that. Trent aims Bill's sperm at the trunk of the brugmansia but it just drops onto the path at their feet with dry tocks. Heaving a stone would make Bill's face more vulnerable but his skinny legs wobble entertainingly. His cock is still so rigid that his arms float out from his hips as though he were stepping back from it.

The cup has disappeared. For a second Trent feels deep shame, that strong reverse gear. As though in a dream, the automatic sprinkler system starts hissing. Time begins again, but with a different rhythm. Trent feels tiny winds when the waspy bees fly close to his face—Bill's bees. Trent finally asks, "Do you ever get stung?" He asks Bill to look under his t-shirt—a bee creeps on his spine.

Before leaving, Trent needs to square the purchase of some *podocarpus* with Twitter. All the doors are locked except, oddly, the front door. Her black stainless steel entryway says Drop Dead but the dining room beckons with the soft complexity of many woods and oily lemon polish. Stately Twitter sits at the table; her silver head and bony shoulders pivot above a little black strapless. Trent hesitates, feeling manly in his awkwardness. He feels called upon to "step up to the plate," whatever that means, but her huge red grin is so fiercely intimate that he steps back instead.

Twitter reads Trent's expression and says "Fuck" without rancor. A tuna sandwich—one exact semicircle missing as though a small muzzle chewed it off—bleeds grease on its paper doily on a gold-rimmed plate next to a wine glass and an empty bottle. Trent bothers to read the label and wishes he could read the label on her dress—the *things* of the rich. For some reason she eats her lunch dressed naked.

The room is chilly and Trent has an impulse to cover her defenseless shoulders. Her gold compact lies next to her sandwich; she opens it quickly as though her bright lips might be naked as well. The familiar surroundings make her drinking seem hopeless. "Fuck, fuck, fuck, fuck," she says to the little round mirror as though contributing to a conversation. "My house is fucked, my friends are fucked, my life is fucked, my son is fucked, my clothes are fucked." Trent spots the white glass cup on the mahogany sideboard. Twitter slops a ray of wine onto the table's dark sheen, then squares her shoulders. "*Fuuuck Fuuuck Fuuuck Fuuuck Fuuuck,*" she bawls as Trent creeps away.

THE UNEXAMINED LIFE

Daryl peels carrots and onions over the sink, sniffling, when he spots his neighbor posing in front of his mirror across the street. When the neighbor's jeans slip down two inches below the band of his white briefs, no waist could be more tender. Perhaps he's from Hong Kong. It's twelve-thirty, early for this ritual. Daryl tiptoes to a little closet window covered by dusty Venetian blinds. From the dark closet, the street is painfully bright. This strong light and shadow somehow involve Daryl in an enigmatic world, even nostalgic.

Wrists on the sill, he adjusts his opera glasses: his neighbor jumps forward thirty feet. The binoculars work better if Daryl keeps one eye closed. The neighbor's thin arms bend backward like fledgling wings, he's looping his belt: eye candy for the cyclops. Then he bends over, just his shoulders visible, so he's making cuffs? When he bends, the television comes into view—miles of densely hued farmscape rush headlong into the still frame. The neighbor straightens up and bends and straightens up; after each adjustment he studies the mirror.

The neighbor bends down, gone; Daryl's closet smells like old cardboard boxes and bank statements; a car alarm goes woowoowoowoowoo: it's boring. The TV eye hurtles over blue and white coast. Daryl watches himself watching. The Oracle orientation left him feeling old enough to retire and stuffed his head with terms like massive reorg and human resources. Yet the experience was also infantilizing: the forced jauntiness, the jokes about when they could use the toilet. Daryl looked around the conference room at the pained faces and the faces lapping it up. There was applause after each presentation. "Failure is not an option. When I hear the word *no*, I get excited," one vice-president affirmed, as though inducting them into a business cult.

His neighbor tips toward his window and cranes forward, way past the fictional plane. Daryl jumps back scalded, slats click downward. He can't resist lifting a slat to see if he's been discovered. What if he has? Was his neighbor unaware all along of the excitement he foments in the opposite building's units? The neighbor's mouth hangs open and his head slides sideways as he peers with all his might through bunched-up eyes. Finally he gives up; he bends over and somehow pulls his pants off from his cuffs. When he stands he's an Asian Marky Mark, round pecs and white briefs, checking his modest basket and trying out a grin on himself. He disappears and comes back hopping into another pair of jeans. He studies himself from the side, glowering up past his brow at his lowered face. From the side he's skinny as a noodle except for his pecs, the fruit of much lifting. Sometimes he exercises the living flesh with free weights wearing only a jockstrap.

Daryl adjusts his binoculars, focusing on the

reflection. He loves flesh loved by its owner, bodies that dispense the confidence needed to love them. He helps himself to the neighbor's excitement. The mirror gives him access, perhaps it makes arousal porous. The neighbor is also aroused by a stranger in the mirror: he looks generic even to himself. The jeans slide down, the Venetian blinds slice off the neighbor's head, only his white-underwear rump appears. Even that drops away.

Bingo! He jumps naked into the frame. It causes an urgent friction in Daryl. He hears his breath thicken. Usually the neighbor dances naked later in the evening, getting ready to go out, loosening up. If Trent were home, he would wonder coldly, "Why sneak around? He's in front of his window— it's a performance." For Daryl the performance isn't complete until viewed by a Peeping Tom who steals his ticket to the show. What good is private life if its performance is free?

Dancing to something in his head, the neighbor yanks himself from one side to the other, then centers himself above his hips like a toreador. He's turning himself *on*: dark hair, flat ass, broad shoulders, long back, long legs a little bowed. He pumps his hips while poking the air with his fingers. Daryl squints at the flopping penis as though the blur were a pattern of Ben-Day dots. He tries to place himself close to his neighbor through the power of sight to make the relation a true one.

A need opens up in Daryl and hollows him

out; it's not pleasant yet it's pleasure. Once upon a time, while drinking hot milk from a nipple, self-preservation equaled arousal. Daryl supposes obsessing on his neighbor started there. Since the neighbor is complete, Daryl's excitement must be inappropriate, so fantasy takes the neighbor's place. Fantasy says Daryl can *maneuver* his neighbor onto sexual pinnacles—cries and grunts. In his fantasy, a body must yield to pleasure caused by Daryl despite what its head thinks or wants. The neighbor's lean butt barely jiggles as Daryl—

IT'S GOTTA LOOK LIKE AN ACCIDENT

A key rattles the lock and Daryl's taut sightlines snap, falling without resistance. By turning away Daryl makes the neighbor vanish with no more consequence than turning off the TV. Trent stands in the hall, tasting the air for signs of Ron. He sets a grocery bag on the counter as Daryl wanders in singing the blues: *"I made you lunch/Now don't forget my name."* Pasta and salad wait on the table. A pot steams up the windows. Daryl bends over it, inhaling the rich cloud of chicken. Although mated for sixteen years, it also seems to Daryl that he and Trent are spinsters, comfortable sisters who never marry, who age under each other's eyes, removed from the world.

"Smells good," says Trent. "What are you doing?"

"Making stock."

Trent replays this exchange in his mind for no reason: I know what making stock is. I know he is making stock. What am I asking? He has a strange feeling about the white glass cup: a confusion of textures melting together in the dark. Daryl pulls at the brown paper bag; he can tell from the size of the bag that trouble lies ahead and wonders if this trouble is related to the beer on Trent's breath. Still, he's mildly shocked when he sees only a baguette, two English cucumbers and a quart of 2% instead of ingredients for dinner. He's isolated by an unwanted insight into his lover's inner workings. Here are the expected fragments, but where is the personality that binds?

Trent protests: "I *took* the shopping list," as though that were the goal. "You *said* we needed bread," as though that were the only need. Trent hates days like this, parties with their tension and toil—and for what? Insincere acting and over-espoused opinions that painfully display ruined egos. He'd rather eat dinner on the sofa with Daryl as they love to do, watching whatever happens to be on TV.

"Fine," says Daryl, putting on a placid mask. He reminds himself, Don't look to a relationship for justice. He asks weakly, "Would you shop after lunch while I cook?"

First Ron, then Francie, now This. One second ago, Trent didn't know how he was spending the afternoon; now his plans are irreversible: eat lunch, smoke dope, jog, take a nap. "I *have* to relax before dinner." He puts wonder into it, slowly shaking his head, speaking to a child. "I'm very *aware* of my limitations and I *cannot* go shopping."

Daryl sees his tasks double. Trent makes grace under pressure seem impossibly limited. He's not a team player, yet the language he uses to justify himself is excruciatingly borrowed. "I don't have time to run around all day—I've got to get my needs met." The phrase *get my needs met* blows in from the void. It angers Daryl more than the extra work.

Daryl looks at Trent, tests for feelings of love. It's not possible to cheat on the test because the test itself is cheating. Trent's face is painful to consider, exaggerated. His stilted defense is made worse by his sincere belief in it. Daryl feels the brunt of chance. It gives him a window on the endless night outside the inevitability of Daryl and Trent. Now their personalities are random circuits guiding but limiting all communication till it can no longer be called communication. The emptiness of communication awes Daryl, as though a god or element were speaking—something too shallow to understand, like weather. He has a vision of the acquisition of all language—citizens joyously putting on their chains.

Trent raises his voice, beating a noisy retreat with his food. "Daryl, just tell me what time you want me home and I will *be* here,"—as though that were all Daryl asked for. Trent's explicit desire to be happy, to put himself at the top of his priorities, is repulsive to Daryl, though that may be Daryl's insecurity, controlling the game of happiness by losing it on purpose. If Daryl pursues a grievance they will fight and the party will be ruined. Trent will not give in; in fact, he enjoys blowing up, it's a rush. Daryl will be Trent's prisoner, easily surrounded and treed by a jubilant assault, a pack of yapping dogs.

Trent lights a joint before eating lunch. Anyway, he reasons, people at parties want what I already have: sex with whoever I like, spectacular looks, and Daryl. Trent buys grass for Daryl from a buyers club but smokes it himself. The human brain makes its own pot, his brain informs itself, adding, Except for grass, recreational drugs no longer seem to jibe with a healthy lifestyle.

    Trent sits on the cane wingback by the bowl, having random thoughts in his agitation: Cleo lives in the United States; she's an American fish living on her own. Yogis pull their eyeballs out and pop them back. He blathers away: Does she miss Francie? Death can be a rewarding experience. Does she see me through the bowl? Or just her reflection? Which she thinks is another Cleo?

IMPRINT OF BELIEF

Preoccupied, frazzled, Daryl steps onto the front porch and mentally exclaims, What a beautiful planet! A warm tender day: Soft air draws whips of clouds slowly into white masses above the horizon and a moon-shell faintly ornaments the blue. Unspeakable joy in the form of gold light falls on the white clapboard of the old house. The light's pulse beats faster than anyone can see or hear. Daryl wants to follow the light but how? What form could he take? Typically he makes a problem: If I allowed myself a longing that great, where would I be?—lost in some tremulous music. My greed keeps me from the day. Really, these insipid thoughts keep me from it—

Daryl is an ant and grasshopper hybrid. The grasshopper believes he will have second and third chances to strengthen his careless relation to life. He makes himself increasingly hopeless promises to return later to fulfill his experiences. He fears giving up childhood and youth because he has not really lived them. Meanwhile, the finality of each moment throws the ant into frantically useless activity.

Daryl drops into his old Toyota. The car is surprisingly hot, the heat empty and prickly. Daryl puts on sunglasses for protection. He bumps the sun visor which leaks powder through a rip in the plastic. He holds his breath as the toxic unknown twinkles in the air.

A funeral drives south on Dolores; Daryl

waits for it to pass. The cars continue even when the light turns red. Death has the right of way—all the way to the graveyard in Colma, Daryl supposes. Most of the cars look old and beat up. Daryl thinks, You almost don't see a burial anymore. Everyone goes up in flames—nothing remains of death but its impurity.

The wind pulls little black flags on the antennas into rigid seizures. The long hearse, the black armbands. The old pomp of death, a procession. It's hard for Daryl to imagine his own death without being dramatic. This serviceable body suddenly becomes completely estranged; age has already begun the process of drilling slow leaks into this boat. It's dragged down by a mighty undertow. A clear bell chimes across the day he's absent from. To contemplate that day is a strange exalting mystery. He misses some link between familiarity and estrangement that would make his death less fantastic. It's a sphinx riddle whose solution lies hidden in the open. A feeling of personal failure? Guilt?

Daryl was diagnosed two years ago; he and Trent went to see Joyce to help them sort out their feelings. They see a female therapist because Trent had an affair with the previous one, Jed, Daryl remembers bitterly. Then he bursts out laughing in spite of himself, savoring the plot at his own expense. The sexy sick man is asymptomatic but the future gives him tremendous stage fright—Daryl has no lines to learn because there is no community self-description for an ageing, unsexy, diseased fag. It makes him tired and tense that he has to go all that way on his own. In his community, fear in the face of death is the sign of a false life. To kill the suspense he could almost hurl his life like a bomb—at who?

The prospect of dying makes Daryl particular to himself, like taking one giant step into middle age. His childhood once conferred meaning on his life, a sort of fatalism of retrospection. Now he looks toward death's tableau. *"Gibraltar may tumble/The Rockies may crumble/But my Death is here to stay."*

He drives on the hot quiet street. Young mayten trees sway softly above their oval shadows. Although Daryl is not a writer or artist, he hopes to finish his "early work" and commence his "mature work." The trees' shadows are like sundials, the visual manifestation of time. He suspects that society is not letting him grow up. Somewhere else adults are deciding about trade deficits, urban renewal, genetic engineering, war and peace.

Daryl turns on Castro (*Arabian Nights* on the theater marquee) and heads south. His car groans tautly on the steep hill—a red VW first seen in the rearview mirror actually passes. At the top, the unprotected white street drops into the next valley and ascends on the other side through a bright jumble of houses, telephone lines, and firs. The blue of the sky is so strong Daryl sees black behind it. Distant hills turn blue-gray. Why is it beautiful?

Daryl lets the clutch out and down he

goes. He drives with a voiceover: When you move to a city, its geography is apparent, bay and hill. That awareness is swamped by a jumble of social intensities that rarely admit an unobstructed view. But San Francisco gives you that unobstructed view, which makes tourists of Daryl and Trent. Daryl also feels that way about Trent; Daryl enjoys the view, but as a tourist.

It's bizarre that Daryl is infected and not Trent. Huh, thinks Daryl, old age would suit me better. How will Trent endure it?—when he can't bring the world to order with his body.

Daryl parks on 24th St. and walks faster than other people. He feels pressure. Cool in the shade, sweaty in the sun, California. He's excited by the street with its coffee fragrance and its windows; he's attracted to things to eat and wear. Men and women carry home food, flowers, dry-cleaning, magazines and newspapers, videotapes and wine. It's nature to Daryl—he'd like to be interred in the cheese store, in the cooler, behind the ripening Gorgonzolas, or down the street at the produce market under the organic melons.

The bakery woman and Daryl laugh when they see each other. They amuse each other. Daryl's deep brow casts a shadow across his amber eyes that causes a tremolo in her chest, partly maternal. She calls him the Girl with the Golden Eyes. The church of the butcher: the martyrs hacked apart and displayed, the fish shaped and colored for an alien world. For a moment Daryl mourns Francie. Francie was like himself, Cleo is like Trent with her fascinating, repulsive narcissism. He wonders if Trent makes that comparison.

At the cheese store, Daryl pauses to breathe, adjusting to the clammy decadence. As Ron's heinous letter said: *Breathing in is witchcraft.* Insanity has a public aspect—it speaks with a language it doesn't own. A couple looks at Daryl, wearing expressions almost comically expectant. A middle-aged couple, oddly familiar. Daryl admires his pointed nose and her disheveled gray bun. Daryl drags his glance away, then swings it back. They stand shoulder to shoulder, hands folded at the waist, foursquare as a Colonial portrait. Daryl can't acknowledge them or interrupt his solitude. He feels remorse but passes by, denying their frank innocence. He casts about for a language to express his fear. He doesn't stop to see if they are disappointed.

He met them in Paris two years ago and enjoyed an hour with them. Are they really that couple? Visiting San Francisco, another tourist destination? On the busy street, Daryl stands against the current feeling warm light push like hands on his shoulders and scalp. He rubs his fuzzy head. Side by side in his cheese store? Memory crowds a crowded city constructed daily out of glances. They were very sweet to Daryl and Trent—for how long?—twenty minutes, an hour and a half? Even extending an invitation—to Leicester? Cambridge?

The rosy odor of strawberries dominates the produce market, fragrance so intense it's an urge. Daryl's senses don't merely find facts—his being shapes itself in textures and smells. Daryl holds ripe fruit and juggles need and price. This part of civilization is more degraded than ever. Still, here are the ancient bins of turnips and carrots, peppers and chard, apples and pears. Daryl rejects the plums, just sacks of water. The tomatoes are wooden except cherry tomatoes. He buys onions, thyme, ginger, cabbage, pears... This onion: already the rushed knife disrupts cells whose lachrymator dissolves in the fluid of the eye; already flame converts the flesh: opaque to lucent, bitter to sweet.

Two wines: a white taut as a harp string; a red for the duck, austere, tasting like dirt and sun.

The day is running through Daryl's fingers. A man waits for the light, rubbing his chin. How can the world be one way and not another way?—As though everything pulses, ready to jump out of its shape, the genetic codes empty as any blueprint. Daryl's eyes cloud to recognize the man: Spike LaRocca, an old flame, what a firecracker! After they decided to break up, Spike hooted *Daryl* like an owl or ghost and Daryl levitated toward him in a finale with sparks. Now here's Spike looking like a Kermit balloon in the Macy's parade: huge, benign, and green.

NONSENSE

Trent has a mother somewhere: he dispatched her by forgiving her. She's like the old country, a culture left behind. Trent is still comfy in the infinite while Daryl digs his dungeon.

    Daryl seems to get away from me. As he falls through calls through nalls through shawls through galls through palls through—lines of nonsense pierce him like spears. This nonsense doesn't touch Trent. I lose Daryl but can't say why.

LES LIAISONS DANGEREUSES

During their recent session, Joyce, with her sticky empathy, appealed to Daryl, "Tell us your *fears*, your *worst-case scenario*." Leaning forward, she frowned encouragement.

Events transpire exactly as Daryl feared: "First, Trent sees someone we both know and doesn't tell me. Second, Trent has unsafe sex."

Shifting on the rickety director's chair, Trent drawled, "Well,—"

Joyce interrupted, "What I'm *hearing* is..."

BEETLE PUDDLE BATTLE

Most fictional characters are energetic; Daryl spends his energy keeping his personality organized and the world in place. He consoles himself: I'll write to them. I have their address somewhere—Leicester? Leeds?

Shopping done, most of the food cooked. Where's Trent? Pounding up the stairs. He's squinting and his lips are parted as though he's still heading into wind; he feels like that. In a black-striped, blue Spandex running suit, he's gasping, sweaty, horsey, and exposed. The bulges make Daryl smile. He reaches for Trent's will and tries to destroy its independence.

"You're inconsiderate," he starts.

"I'm auto-considerate." Trent breathes hard, his mouth sucking air. Sweat darkens his blond hair and mats it to his forehead. He kicks off his Nikes and Daryl allows their cheesy smell to please him. "I'm better than you...at getting my needs met...but I haven't been happy...in this relationship...for two years."

A chemical fire travels a silvery high note along Daryl's ribs. He has to sit down. He thinks: *This is the grip of fear.* He settles back, marveling, assimilating the bursts of adrenaline. In the midst of chaos, a rational voice explains, "Trent doesn't love you anymore." It's almost a relief.

"We're not growing together," Trent adds.

"Growing?"

Trent is tearfully sincere and spandex-naked, as though displaying to Daryl what he will soon lack access to. Daryl is stumped. He thinks, If I could just be allowed into Trent's body once more, allowed to have that experience. Then Daryl reminds himself that Trent is probably repeating lines from the Romance Channel. As though to confirm this, Trent cries, "Let's separate before we come to hate each other." Scavenged materials. Trent's rhetoric used to come from pornography; Daryl measures the distance between the eighties and nineties. Daryl has also changed over time but feels deprived of a witness.

Reading Daryl's mind, Trent replies, "You don't even like me." Daryl's jaw actually drops. He feels wrongness he can't express: Trent is making a good point that is somehow beside the point. Daryl feels a marriage-induced disgust for Trent's sexuality. Familiarity reveals it: arbitrary, obvious, ravening. Daryl is nauseated and fatigued, a victim of sunstroke. How to endure, how to forgive Trent's libido?—a stubborn despot, an airy jumble of mismatched psychic debris. They both know Trent will never choose to leave Daryl, but Daryl fears that once embarked on, a story of loss becomes irresistible.

"How do you mean, not growing?"
"Not growing? I never said that."
"You said it one second ago."

Trent steps backward and his jaw drops. "That's crazy. I could *never* say *anything* like that. I said, 'I need to spend more time alone.'"

"*Alone?*" Daryl goes insane for a moment, but no one keeps a journal of record and Trent has no commitment to the past. Daryl grabs Windex from below the sink and pumps at the window with ammoniacal fury. Trent says, "What are you doing?" and Daryl raises his hands in mock bewilderment. Trent needs a catharsis and can't process Daryl's retreat. He blames HIV.

Has Daryl ever been *in* love with Trent?— Daryl attains the distance to wonder. In their early twenties they were two parts of an easy puzzle, their satisfaction a complete picture. They experienced each other through the imagination. Now imagination is the barrier that keeps them apart. It's not a change in them, but in the meaning of imagination. How far would he have to "back up" from Trent in order to fall in love?

ARRAY

The day delivers itself to Ron as though the heat wave burned off a skin of resistance. Ron has a long sheep face, long black sausage curls, and he wears a brown overcoat for some reason. His cheeks are too red, burning medals. In the aroused twilight, he watches patiently from the shelter of willed invisibility above their garden on a hill. Trent is Ra, the gaudy sun, who long ago impregnated Ron through anal intercourse. Drone of a helicopter. That's why the only thing an alien fetus wants is chocolate. Thunk of car doors. The Egyptian rulers were aliens (their elongated heads). Coins of late sunlight fall through swags of climbing roses and the branches of the old prune plum, a few plums purple in the leaves. The shadow of the chaise's slats not falling but still, all other shadows rolled by the wind.

Time convexes on itself, contracting to a single point as the unconscious and the conscious trade places. AIDS changes people into dolphins as human evolution returns us to the ocean (land is ruined). Suddenly a forlorn yellow light shines overhead, a window.

Ron becomes the rough edge of Styrofoam on the lip, the heat in the throat and the flavor on the tongue. He peels back shiny foil and takes a bite, melts with it. Chocolate for the alien fetus. The ching of a bicycle bell. Peeling paint exposes gray patches on the fenders and doors of Trent's old green truck. Slash the tires, pour sugar in the tank, acid on the hood? These alternatives have a high succinct wit. Ron's head rolls in deep amusement as though the fight against evil were brilliant repartee. A Black man in a suit strides downhill with a newspaper tucked under his arm. Ron calls, "Hey man, I freed your people." The man crosses the street. Ron's shadow against the fence. The powerless clouds.

Long ago, Ron touched flesh from a different order. Beauty gave that flesh the independence of mathematics, no shame inside and out. Now that very lack of shame makes Trent responsible—for what? For casting shadows. Trent did not even listen when Ron begged for help. Ron may be nuts, but he sees as though in plain view that he will die alone, killed by the city. They won't let him dish up slices at Marcello's forever. Ron *is* an artist. Trent is the enemy of art because he has no conscience. Even his shadow enrages Ron.

Now clouds descend toward night and moths flicker in the trees. Goodbye gaudy sun, how can a ghost look at you? Birds roost in the branches, their spirits withdraw with the day. What is day to them now? Nefertiti was vain so the aliens killed her, but not before she cursed humankind. Her curse brought on the patriarchy; her curse is language itself that breaks our consciousness in two. The sky and earth are separate mirrors, gods and humans are separate mirrors. All myths are one: the separation of man and god.

Daryl and Trent appear on the back deck. They are a couple. Their good luck becomes Ron's bad luck. They are not only flesh but the incarnation of Ron's exalted contempt: an aging Muscle System pretty boy and his gloomy husband, a schlub in a pricey shirt who's straining the seams of his slacks. Men his age wear skin-tight pants because they refuse to buy a larger waist. Ron snorts with distaste. Choking his voice, he says "Fucking Nazis."

Trent turns around, feeling pressure. "Oh," he says, "Matt called up—he can't come." Daryl declines to reply, but he's relieved to see his dinner through one less pair of eyes, in particular those of his future boss. Daryl sweeps, Trent waters tomatoes and basil. Ron wants Trent to mention his letter. Life is boring for a stalker. Ron tips his head back and squints as though they are the criminals. What can Ron do to combat Trent's power?

Trent tries to get back on track with Daryl, takes an interest. "What can we put the bread in that's easy to pass around?"

"Your butthole," Daryl replies, deliberately toneless.

"Daryl!" Trent's quick survey: the innocent couple next door, the demented psychiatrist above, Albie below, the exhibitionist across the street— none within earshot. Meanwhile Ron leans against a cream fender in plain sight once you know how to see him. In his apartment in the Tenderloin, he heals the curse of Nefertiti by setting two mirrors facing each other. On one of the mirrors he taped *Leontyne Price: The Prima Donna Collection*, and on the other Nancy Wilson's *Today My Way*; between them he placed a can of tuna, on top of that a shell—an antenna to send information to aliens. Ron recognizes himself in the culture's grand anxieties. He plays the dolphinlike music of Oval's *Systemisch*.

"I hope the delphiniums last till they come," Trent offers, as though he and Daryl were conversing. "I'll cut some roses?" Trent gathers carnations, sweetpeas, and tiny Sweetheart buds from the heavy canes.

Ron thinks, "When I turn the craters of the moon inside out, I see red and no bubbling white light. I have to conjure that up, build it from the inside out until I see it."

SLIPPAGE THE CLOWN

The guests are due in ten minutes and Daryl is blunted by fear. In his chest thuds the certainty that he *must* set the table and reduce the sauce before they arrive. He locates a bottle of port in the cabinet and splashes the pan hysterically. His determination blots out thought. When the doorbell finally chimes, Trent rushes down—a host at last, to Daryl's great relief. Daryl hears the tread on the stairs and compartmentalizes his terror in a mighty act of will. It's Bill the butler and a stranger. Daryl thinks, How like Trent's friends to bring uninvited guests to small dinners. In this instance, a deerlike youth who stirs a flurry of lust in the men. Because of the deer-youth, Daryl can see the maturity in Trent's face which equals the time they lived together.

    Daryl waits at the top with the exquisitely critical graciousness of Clarissa Dalloway while mentally redistributing the food. Is bringing a deer-youth like bringing wine or flowers? Or a bone? Daryl asks, "Who's da tomata?" Bill introduces Toddy. Toddy is a dancer; a hank of brown hair frames a simple face whose teeth look like one gleaming block of sugar. He retails sunglasses by day, an expanding industry. He's twenty-three and calls his orgasms me-flowers.

    "I'm fine," says Peg before anyone can greet her. She walks ahead like a pigeon with straight little legs. She rubs Daryl's head, a soft brush high above her. "How's your health?"

"Nothing to report." Daryl appreciates Peg.

Steven's forehead furrows in horizontal lines equidistant as a musical staff. He resembles Clark Kent, stolid, inert. Beneath that mild manner lies an ever-breaking heart. He's a little dressy in his brown tweed jacket. Trent can tell Peg and Steven just made love: her face vibrates and he looks emptied out. They came until they saw stars, Trent informs himself. They offer a Côtes du Rhône and for Steven a bottle of Snapple. Toddy is a vegetarian but can graze around the flesh.

When Daryl presents the platter of duck legs braised with cabbage and red onion, the guests look up from the table with delight and gratitude, a moment Daryl pictured, longed for all day—all his life. A thread of grassy thyme runs through the dark sweet fragrance. Their mouths water as Daryl makes a ceremony of handing each guest a plate heavy with food. The duck is amazingly tender, the rich dull meat suffused with thyme, the vegetables deeply caramelized. The wine tastes like a Band-Aid, as Côtes du Rhônes often do.

Toddy says, "I couldn't live if I had to live by killing others."

"For his last meal, the murderer James Smith asked for a lump of dirt," Daryl remarks.

"Dirt is not a vegetable," Toddy claims, a question in his voice.

"You mean eating meat?" Peg asks. "Where

would you stop?—life is founded on brutality. What could you hold up against that?" She holds up her dainty fingers. Beneath her black cowboy shirt her breasts still feel the rasp of pleasure.

As though to reply, Bill says: Toddy was at Burning Man.

Steven: Burning Man?

Toddy: You know, in the desert?

Daryl: What was there?

Toddy: Things you couldn't describe!

Trent: Describe them.

Toddy: Everything you can think of. It was unbelievable.

Steven: What was unbelievable?

Toddy: You name it!

Peg: Name what?

Toddy: Oh, just everything!

The guests look on in disbelief. Daryl rejoices. His love for their shiny expressive faces stretched tight in the soft cone of light wells up as a tremolo in his chest and thighs. His guests speak, reply: the least act of communication is a miracle and miracles abound.

They talk about: gay rodeos vs. animal rights activists (Peg); transsexuals as the new royalty of the bar scene, "the holy place of gender differentiation" (Toddy); acid replacing ecstasy (Bill) (it *never* does); the X chromosome's gay gene discovered in the brains of forty-one men and a few castrated rats (Steven); Nirvana at the Cow Palace raising money for Bosnian rape victims (Toddy—with the zeal of the recently briefed). A lesbian couple wants a sperm donor commitment from Steven but they are cagey about what they are offering. Will Steven and Peg have a baby? "We've been together three months," Peg protests.

After a smoldering bartender named Gino dropped Steven's heart, it rebounded at Peg, a hot baby butch-dyke with a blond crew cut, a small square brow and small polished ears. She tends Steven's sorrow, a marvelous bloom. She's so male and dead-on that all the men flirt with her. She's a performance artist; in her new work a soul leaves a body as though in broken friendship. In three weeks she will take her show to New York. Paraphrasing Liza, she sings, "If I *fail* there, I've failed *every*where."

There is so much food and wine that the guests begin to suffer. The tops of their stomachs bulge, they are too aware that heads sit on necks, sight perches on faces that wrap around memories. They idly shove knives and forks through the woven straw placemats (horrified, Daryl does not know how to stop them) while insulting their partners in cosmic exasperation.

Steven complains that Peg talks to herself, giving herself directions. "That's a Cancer: totally emotional with a controlling center."

"What about Capricorns?" Peg counters. "A whole race of Do-Me Queens." Daryl wonders if their experimental union is showing cracks. Each confided to him proudly that Peg fucks Steven with a dildo.

Daryl says about Trent, "It's no good discussing an idea with a Leo. For a Leo to even consider someone else's opinion is the same as losing control."

"You think Cancers are emotional, try Pisces," says Toddy about Bill. "They're just bags of water. Total sex addicts. They can't tell the truth because safety exists only in ambiguity."

Except for Toddy, the guests don't believe in astrology. Toddy augmented his knowledge with "rumpology," an art he learned from a Frenchwoman. "The crack of your ass corresponds to the two hemispheres of the brain," he says. "The buttocks represent areas of your personality. The rump is divided into four quadrants, air, fire, water and earth..."

"So as you age your future sags?" Daryl asks, to carry the subject further. But Toddy has come to the limit of his knowledge. Eyeing the couples with hostility, Daryl wonders if they all quarreled before dinner.

Toddy seems to know Bill very well, Trent observes with a mild pang. Trent has a pressing memory: he's penetrating Bill doggy-style when Bill, in his excitement, grabs the pillow in his teeth and shakes it from side to side like a dog. What a moron. How long have they been seeing each other? Trent is drinking too much wine so more drinking is necessary, a kind of destination. For some reason Trent imagines setting the white glass cup on the long white tablecloth of the Last Supper. The cup breaks the fictional plane but not forever.

"Medical experts say it is healthy, a sign of mental health, to talk to yourself," Trent informs Steven about Peg.

"That's so not true," Daryl snaps. "I love Trent's instant science." Trent launches a mock-attack, holding Daryl's big neck and batting his head like a plugged-up ketchup bottle, the gesture wide from drink.

"If you love it so much why don't you marry it?" Bill quotes Pee-wee Herman.

"It's annoying!" says Daryl, meaning, You're annoying.

"If it's so annoying why don't you marry it?" Trent sneers from the sink. The Pacific Rim's sleek highlights spill over the dishes in his hands; silverware clatters vehemently. Trent bristles with accuracy: alcohol lights that part of his mind. He barks orders at Daryl—"Bring the plates!" "Fill the glasses!"—marking a stage of drunkenness. Daryl looks around: the chaos of all relationships. He feels sick—instead of inspiring each other, his guests isolate themselves.

Trent calls, "Hey Daryl, your little honey is taking off his clothes."

The living room has the best view. United once more, the dinner guests crowd around the window. "Mmmmmm," Bill groans, "I could swallow him in two bites and still be hungry." Steven also thinks (in his own gloomy register), The boy eats the world, now I eat the boy.

Trent complains, "On weekends he blasts the same dumb song over and over—what an idiot."

"Everybody's *freeeeeeeeeeeee* to feel good..." Daryl prances in place while touching his beatific face with all his fingertips: ecstasy (the drug).

The guests cry out in unison when the neighbor pulls down his briefs. His thin cock and big black patch. He gathers their attention, creating a psychic trade deficit. Trent scorns that prosperity and feels superior to Daryl. He informs the guests in a cold femmy voice that every man in the building gawks at the exhibitionist without a qualm while Daryl creeps around with binoculars, turning off lights.

Daryl says very piously, "The unexamined life is not worth living!"

Bill defends Daryl, smirking. "Twitter likes to watch."

Trent hazards, "Oh? Does she drink from a glass cup while she watches?"

Bill considers this, mouth ajar, eyes round and shallow. He backs slowly across the room saying, "Wait a minute, wait a minute..." till his calves hit the couch and he plops backward. It's so subtly inappropriate that Trent wonders if he's dreaming. He's pushed for a moment into dizzy wine-laced sleep. Trent is afraid the cup will vanish like a dream but he doesn't know a way to remember it. The cup breaks his consciousness, but not irreversibly. He awakes with the knowledge that Bill stages sex shows for Twitter under the brugmansia. Bill says, "Twitter's the kind of person who owes a big apology to everyone she meets."

A third or fourth bottle appears. Trent scrubs his numb face with both hands. It seems everyone has brought a piece of information. So many are needed.

Bill: Twitter had an operation and her son Bobo pissed her doctor off. Bobo kept saying, "No extraordinary measures—nothing heroic to keep Twitter alive." It was just knee surgery.

Peg, gathering them with her eyes: Tex's family could not deal with his death. The last words he heard were his brother asking, "Hey, want to watch *Antiques Roadshow*?"

Toddy (his fingers submerging in the orange pad of Bill's hair): When someone shoves a few tabs of acid in your butt you're called a punch bowl. Then people get high fucking and rimming you.

Steven (with always fresh surprise deepening the lines on his brow): I get his name tattooed on my fucking arm and all he gives me is a little hug.

Steven finds elaborate excuses to reinstate his fickle bartender (or preserve his absence)—*Gino* runs in cursive script across his forearm as though engraved on a silver frame in which the photo declines to appear. Steven hacked into Gino's chatrooms and methodically had sex with eight of Gino's partners. Steven pleads, "Is that how he *always* was? Was he *always* going to have sex with every twinkie who comes along?" If he proves that Gino is "wrong," there's hope that Gino can "reform" and return Steven's love, which is "right." This logic is the last resort of the badly loved, argued before friends, the court of last resort. Steven's small portion of sociability is used up. He wears a dazzled expression, legs widespread. Peg jigsaws the curve of herself, pressing the top of her little black Converse into his calf and kneading his arm with fond possession.

A molten burnt-sugar hatred surges in Trent. He sits forward with hands on his knees as though dispensing justice: Go, go, go, go, he chants mentally. He's next to Cleo; she's as shallow as his guests. Her mouth detaches and pushes out when she breathes and she's like that; her face disunites for a repulsive instant of sexual ugliness, like an insect made of parts independently whirring. Trent turns to Daryl for help but Daryl doesn't notice that their party is falling apart. He sits jumbled on a butterfly chair, his mouth and arms jerk like a puppet's. Daryl needs to talk, a compulsion strong as passionate love.

Trent wants to go home but he's already there. Why don't his guests feel the same? Peg and Steven are dismal pan-faced American Gothics waiting for the train—will it ever come? Peg crosses her feet.

Trent rubs his brow. He can't feel his nose when he touches it and that makes him laugh. How to interpret the evening? A dumb comedy, but each laugh is a sob racked from his body. He begins crying without grief. Tears restore his sense of scale. Tears are glasses allowing him to focus. Trent slides bonelessly to the floor and unfurls sideways on the Chinese rug with the grace of the truly drunk. He raises his eyes, "What can I do now?"

Everything is impossibly broken—he hacks out the hard tears. If his self-control holds the world together, the world must fall apart. He cries in deep surrender, his face is purple, he's imploring ballad-style—for what? Through tears and mucous, he says, "She matched the castle!" As though he knows what he's saying.

The guests freeze in gestures of dismay as though Trent were a lamp that crashed over. Perhaps they would be more shocked if they were not drinking, except for Steven, hooked on grief but emphatically sober. He never *had* a problem with alcohol, but who would dare day it?

Daryl draws Trent into his arms to absorb the shock. If you accept someone's love you are responsible for him—is that ethics? Daryl says, "Go put water on your face." In the tense room, Daryl can hear his own stagy voice as though on tape, the wind whistling in electronic ravines. I'm a queen, he notes with alarm. Trent allows himself a bitter thought: he means I'm a fish. Daryl's suggestion steadies Trent; he turns to the guests, falls into their arms one by one to cry a little, parsing out the last of his sorrow.

Trent talks himself in: Step around Peg's foot, turn the knob. He holds the jamb and bows, backing into the bathroom. The latch catches: click. The unbearable drone of the swarm dissolves in effervescent silence that seems to ascend. Trent hangs onto the sink while silence starts revolving gruelingly. He looks to the mirror for ballast. Bruised circles beneath his eyes, vampire skin, swollen lips, heavy blond hair tangled in bed-head perfection. "Wow," he thinks, "I look airbrushed!"

Even though Trent is alone, he feels his face drawing desire to it. Trent sees orgasms firing pop-pop-pop-pop-pop like flashbulbs of the paparazzi emitting a light to bathe in, a light that resembles health, sheer physical release that rings in new life and relates his tension outward. His flesh is not all flesh but partly the lust it generates. He attracts himself by proxy. He runs his thick tongue around the inside of his mouth—that feeling belongs to him. But other people share the arousal in his groin, nipples and lips, and the feeling on the skin of his butt, the satin knot, the pressure inside, the touched membranes ready to be touched again.

When the guests thank Daryl for a pleasant evening, he stares dumbfounded and dredges up polite clichés with visible effort. By the time the pleurant emerges, the guests have gone.

It's one o'clock. Daryl brushes his teeth. He knows what Trent was doing all that time in the bathroom—Trent left his reflection in the mirror. It supersedes Daryl's own and he feels a pang of love.

Daryl is already under the covers when Trent comes in from the garden. He was looking for signs of Ron.

BACKWARD LAND

Daryl wakes up. It's still night; something is wrong. His body feels okay. Wind rattles the windows, the clock ticks heavily, a song goes through his mind: "After the Ball Is Over." He idly thinks, If the sound of one car is overtaken by the sound of another car they are talking to each other.

He hears a thunk that makes him look at the clock—4 a.m. He smells chemical fumes. From Trent? That's not the right sound or smell. There's a clanking on the steps, the garage door rattles. He's waited for years to hear these wrong sounds. He zips and buttons with trembling fingers. He rasps, "Trent, get up."

Trent sits up. "Huhhh?" though he already knows.

Red enamel drips down the terrazzo stairs. The empty can stands in a red puddle on the porch. Daryl reaches the street as Trent shoots past him, running in all directions at once. No one walks by, yet Trent spins around with his hands raised to ward off the next assault. Big red swastikas cover the garage door. Albie edges downstairs around the paint, the dome of his shaved head a welcome sight. He's always awake at this hour, dedicated to the work of grieving.

Daryl exclaims, "Nice shoes!"

Albie explains, "One advantage when your lover dies is you get his clothes."

Daryl and Trent don't want the neighbors to see Ron's handiwork though they couldn't say why. Thank god the paint is still wet. Trent finds some turpentine in the basement, stored in the landlord's painting supplies. Albie swabs the stairs while Daryl and Trent work side by side on the door, scrubbing the swastikas with turpentine-soaked rags, shedding their fatigue as they sweat in the cold fumes.

The empty street is bright but they set up a few more lights, turning the sidewalk into a room. Daryl feels close to Trent now that he's been attacked, a heightened awareness of Trent's tender body in the rough clothes and cold air. He's glad Trent ruined their party. He's grateful for the...*texture* that Trent supplies. Daryl almost laughs; he still has the opportunity to pivot Trent's dazzling head toward intimacy, to cherish Trent's skin by pressing it against his own. Daryl thinks of a train station with its gusts of warmth and cold, excitement and boredom, arrivals and departures, light-spangled darkness, baggage and freedom. What a strange joy: here in the backward world, something abrasive and cleansing.

SPLIT THE DIFFERENCE

Daryl returns to bed but Trent keeps watch from their windows. Finally he peels the sweaty blue shirt and wrinkled slacks off his fresh skin. He emits a whiff of turpentine. His cock cantilevers outward and swings on its own. He places Daryl's hand across it.

"Your pee-pee's blue," Daryl observes.

"Not getting enough circulation?" Trent wonders.

"Thank you, God, for this special bit of skin," Daryl prays, rolling the most sensitive patches on Trent and on himself between his thumbs and fingers.

"You're welcome, Sucker," Daryl replies in God's baritone. "My whole body is covered in skin like that."

Daryl gratefully turns off the light: "No no no no," Trent cries in a finicky voice, "I can't find the bed!"

"Use your nose," Daryl advises and farts: toot! Trent's rich laughter. Daryl can always get him with a fart joke. The room is not very dark.

Trent pleads, "All I want is for us to lie down together and be together." A sudsy moment from the Romance Channel?

Daryl holds his face above Trent's, mingling alcohol and toothpaste. When they kiss a dam bursts and saliva gushes from Trent's mouth. Daryl drinks it, repulsed. They are too tired but they have sex anyway. It doesn't mean much. They keep dozing off, then building up new arousal only to have it collapse. The current of consciousness twinkles when it breaks, then the thudding black ride and the tiny lurch when they wake an instant later in slightly different places. Somehow Daryl is jacking off Trent and harassing the tiny insensitive nipples that cap his pecs.

As pumping Trent's "awesome member" goes from play to work, Daryl blames Trent: *He's* the one who wants sex; no charwoman scrubbing stones *endures* such drudgery. Here in the center of marriage a shutting down, disgust. Unwanted pleasure is like a histamine attack, an allergic reaction. Long ago, Trent's sexuality seemed coherent. Now it seems haphazard and flawed. Daryl looks at Trent's body without lust—pities its vulnerability, what it hopes to achieve.

As Trent's arousal progresses, he feels Daryl's familiar body gaining mystery and the arbitrary deepens into need. Even though Trent only holds Daryl's cock in his hand, Trent's own pleasure is organized around it. Happy wife!—he feels pleasantly unworthy. Pleasure, a mild shock, pulls the plug on sound and leaves a high note.

Daryl turns Trent around and blows him, one arm supporting Trent's arching waist, the other around his rump, as though taking him with burning kisses like a silent movie sheik. Daryl's own pantomime excites him.

Who penetrates who?—it's decided by the slightest gesture, a lifted thigh. Trent's knock-knees and wide hips offer access, like an idea come to fruition: an erection and a butt. "Shall I put my pee-pee in your rumpus room?" Trent snorts and climbs on his hands and knees. Where's a condom? When does Trent feel naked?—with his butt in the air and Daryl plunging into the surprising heat that *is* Trent? It matters to Daryl whether Trent's spine is turned under, a dog cringing beneath a whipping, or tipped up and open in lavish greed. Daryl recognizes the sweet fetid vapor. On the other end, Trent's head swivels and whispers, "Slam it in harder." His head looks too big and complex above his smooth back and rump.

"What?" Daryl doesn't believe his ears or his luck.

"Harder, please." The bony husband gives his ample wife a drubbing that makes her flesh jiggle, her butt lift, and the bed creak monumentally. Drops of sweat swing off Daryl's face onto Trent's skin. Although Daryl penetrates Trent, he seems to gather Trent into him. Now it takes sex to float the mind through another's body. Who knows where energy comes from at this time of night?

Because Daryl *absorbs* Trent, he knows what Trent feels. First ouch ouch ouch ouch—then a vast space opens inside, filled with pleasure yet empty. A vault so big that another Trent does backflips through clouds like an acrobat. Trent thinks, "This will never end, never never end." Trent begins groaning, a sound Daryl waits for, loose deep growls from an entirely different register, the opposite of blondness, the strain of grinding gears. The oracle speaks an inorganic language.

Trent turns on his back so he can see what is forging through his insides so exquisitely. Framed by his own upturned legs, Trent views Daryl's top half: amber eyes and butterscotch skin, a thick torso decked out in gym muscles and glossy black fur. Trent wonders, How can perfection be unknown to itself? Trent looks into the widening gulf between Daryl and Daryl's flesh, his glory and his fragility.

To arouse himself, Daryl imagines people crowding round the door. What if his body disappoints them? Daryl fantasizes against intimacy, or maybe it's his way of being unfaithful? Now he's sloppy, panting and groaning. His thrusting slides Trent back and forth on the skin of his back. Daryl's orgasms are no longer like climbing, more like being dragged up and over. At the highest point he tips back his churning face and sobs, surprising both of them with some sadness in flesh itself. Daryl allows himself to cry but not to think it solves anything.

Trent bases his orgasm on his affection for Daryl. An orgasm based on love—a whole unexplored direction since it seems to include the past. Amidst convulsions, Trent places his palm on Daryl's chest in tender, Victorian trust. Daryl reads the watery drops on Trent's milky neck and the wooden headboard like tea leaves (except he's telling the past). "By the distance I see you were excited, but there's not much here—you had an orgasm today?"

Trent says, "The arms of the swastikas were backwards, just like in his letter."

Drunk on fatigue, Daryl stares at the ceiling, unable to move, yet imagining an even greater joy and wondering in his poverty of feeling if he mistakes a partial love for a complete one. It's a problem—how do you measure experience? The answer leaves him without a toehold: the only justice you can give experience is to inhabit it completely.

"So we aren't breaking up?" he asks.

"What are you talking about? We're Daryl and Trent."

Daryl floats empty as a box kite. Day begins softly, the air acquires birdsong and the occasional roar of a car climbing. The trees become silhouettes whose branches stir in animated conversation and then subside. Trent curls into Daryl, rubbing his butt against Daryl's crotch. Daryl whispers, "Shhhhhh," as though Trent's motion were sound. Sleep shifts downwards, slipping sideways. Trent says, "You put too much ginger in the pears."

Daryl has the last word. "Shhhhhh, we're post-orgasmic." Trent drifts off and Daryl jacks off quietly, as he often does after sex, to claim the experience and to pour the last drop out of the cistern. They sleep urgently annealed to each other. Although they don't know it, this is the secret of their success. Since the seventies when the myth of Daryl and Trent became flesh and blood, they have spent every night glued skin to skin, de-charging the fury of the day.